Your Dad Was Just Like You

by Dolores Johnson

MACMILLAN PUBLISHING COMPANY   NEW YORK

MAXWELL MACMILLAN CANADA   TORONTO

MAXWELL MACMILLAN INTERNATIONAL   NEW YORK   OXFORD   SINGAPORE   SYDNEY

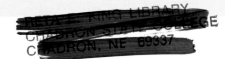

Macmillan Publishing Company is part of the Maxwell Communication Group of Companies. Macmillan Publishing Company, 866 Third Avenue, New York, NY 10022. Maxwell Macmillan Canada, Inc., 1200 Eglinton Avenue East, Suite 200, Don Mills, Ontario M3C 3N1. First edition. Printed in the United States of America. The text of this book is set in 14 pt. Usherwood Book. The illustrations are rendered in watercolor and colored pencil on paper.   10 9 8 7 6 5 4 3 2 1

Library of Congress Cataloging-in-Publication Data. Johnson, Dolores. Your dad was just like you / written and illustrated by Dolores Johnson. — 1st ed.   p.   cm. Summary: While visiting his grandfather, Peter hears a story about his father's boyhood that helps him understand his father. ISBN 0-02-747838-6 [1. Fathers and sons—Fiction. 2. Grandfathers—Fiction.] I. Title. PZ7.J631635Yo 1993   [E]—dc20 92-6347

For my father

Peter stood at the front door of his grandfather's house. "You're the best grandpa that ever was," he said. "Can I move in with you?"

"Move in with me? What happened this time? Did you and your dad have another fight?" asked Peter's grandfather. "You two are always battlin'."

"I wasn't doin' anything, Grandpa," said Peter. "I was just playing around—you know—running, and that ole stupid purple thing on Dad's dresser just seemed to jump onto the floor and break. Dad was so mad, he didn't even yell. He was so mad, he just walked away. Grandpa, I think I need to move in with you."

"Why don't we take a walk, Grandson, and sort this problem out? Sometimes my head works better when my legs get a chance to stretch."

   The two walked through the neighborhood their family had lived in for years. After they had walked some, Peter sighed, "I wish Dad was more like you, Grandpa. He never smiles—he only yells. 'Look at these awful grades, Peter.' 'You never finish anything you start, Peter.' 'Why can't you be more serious, Peter?' He just never leaves me alone."

   "There was a time when your father laughed and smiled all the time," said Peter's grandfather. "When he was a boy, your dad was just like you."

"My daddy was a *boy*…just like *me*?" asked Peter.

"That boy would tell me silly jokes just like you tell. When I didn't even feel like smiling, that boy sure could make me laugh. All he had to do was tell his favorite knock knock jokes."

"*My* dad told *knock knock* jokes?" asked Peter. "You sure you're talking about *my* dad?"

"I know it's hard for you to believe," said his grandfather, "but when your father was young, he was like any other boy. Sometimes he played so long at this park, I almost had to drag him home. He played basketball on that court until he almost wore out the net. He even led big game safaris through that jungle gym."

"Dad played in *my* jungle?" asked Peter.

"He played combat with little green army men on the grass by those swings. He practically wore a groove in this sidewalk with his bicycle. But there was one thing that boy loved to do more than anything else in the world."

"What's that, Grandpa?" Peter chuckled. "Yell at the little kids? Start fights?"

"More than living, laughing, or eating, your father loved to run. He ran from sunup to sundown. He ran so fast that his shadow had trouble keeping up with him."

Peter asked, "So why doesn't my dad run now?"

"There came a time when he became serious. And he told himself, a serious man doesn't run."

"Did he ever run in a race?" asked Peter. "Did he ever win a prize?"

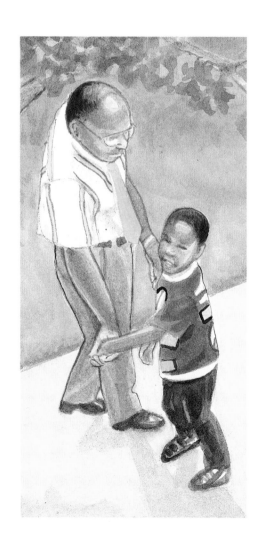

"Your father ran only one race, when he wasn't much older than you. It was the biggest race in the town for schoolkids. Your father sure wanted to win that big golden trophy."

"Dad must have lost the race, 'cause I've never seen any big golden trophy. At least not on the bookshelf where he keeps all his special stuff."

"Sometimes you don't compete for trophies just to place them high up on a shelf," said his grandfather. "Sometimes you compete so you can prove something to yourself. When your father was your age, he had something to prove. He was having trouble in school. Nothing seemed to be going right for him."

"But my daddy's so smart!" said Peter.

"He didn't think he was smart, but he *knew* he was fast. He could run like the wind, and he wanted to show everyone. He stopped playing games. He stopped laughing and joking. He ran day and night as fast as he could because he wanted to run that race and win."

"Did he win, Grandpa?"

Peter's grandfather laughed. "Are you going to let me tell my story? Everyone from town—hundreds of people—lined every inch of that one-mile course to the courthouse. About fifty boys and girls gathered at the starting line, fidgeting and milling about like pigeons on a telephone wire. The starter raised his gun. 'On your mark…get set…' he thundered. And then the worst thing that could possibly happen happened."

"What, Grandpa?"

"A drop of rain fell, and then another and another."

"It started raining?" laughed Peter. "So? I've run a million times in the rain."

"Not rain like this, boy. I looked up, and the sky had turned dark and angry. Rain poured down, and pools of water formed at my feet. The starter didn't have to say 'Go!' because the children had already started running. But they weren't running to the finish line. They were trying to find the last dry spot on earth."

"So Daddy ran for cover too, huh, Grandpa? You know, he doesn't like to mess up his clothes."

"No. It seems your father had something he just had to do. He picked up one leg after the other and ran as fast as he could toward the end of the race. And he kept running even though the rain came down so heavy it nearly knocked him down with its force. The wind howled around him, and pools of water were reaching up to drag at his feet."

"Did Daddy ever reach the finish line?"

"Yes, Grandson, but no one was there to congratulate him. No one handed him a big trophy. No one told him how good he was."

"Where were you, Grandpa?"

"I ran behind your father. I didn't catch up to him until the very end. I finally reached him as he stood alone, shaking his head and sobbing in the rain."

"So what did you do, Grandpa?"

"I picked your father up and carried him home. I dried him off and laid him down. And while he probably cried himself to sleep, I sat down with these two big, clumsy hands of mine and made my boy a trophy, because he really deserved one."

"So where is the trophy now, Grandpa?"

"Well, it…it was…" said the old man.

"Was it a big ole stupid purple…? Oh, I'm sorry, Grandpa. What did Dad say when you gave it to him?"

"He didn't really say much at all…just, 'I love you, Dad,' for the very first time. You see, when your father was a boy, he and I used to fight a lot. I used to yell at him. I hardly ever smiled. We decided to change what was wrong between us. That day, we became a real serious father and son."

"I've got to go home now, Grandpa. There's something serious I've got to do," said Peter. He hugged his grandfather tightly, and then ran the short distance home.

When Peter got home, he gathered the purple pieces that still lay in a heap in his father's bedroom. Then the boy brought them to his own bedroom and worked very hard to make what was broken whole again.

Peter stood in the doorway of the living room and watched his father read in silence. Then the little boy said just three words, even though he was so nervous he felt like running away. "Knock, knock, Dad."

His father hesitated for just a moment, looked up, smiled, and said, "Who's there?"

I Love you Dad